The Secret Garden
Spring Version

Book and Lyrics by
Marsha Norman

Music by
Lucy Simon

A SAMUEL FRENCH ACTING EDITION

SAMUEL FRENCH
FOUNDED 1830

NEW YORK HOLLYWOOD LONDON TORONTO

SAMUELFRENCH.COM

ISBN 978-0-573-69759-3   Printed in U.S.A.   #29200

RENTAL MATERIALS

An orchestration consisting of a **Piano/Conductor Score and Vocal Chorus Books** will be loaned two months prior to the production ONLY on the receipt of the Licensing Fee quoted for all performances, the rental fee and a refundable deposit.

Please contact Samuel French for perusal of the music materials as well as a performance license application.

IMPORTANT BILLING AND CREDIT REQUIREMENTS

All producers of *THE SECRET GARDEN – SPRING VERSION must* give credit to the Author of the Play in all programs distributed in connection with performances of the Play, and in all instances in which the title of the Play appears for the purposes of advertising, publicizing or otherwise exploiting the Play and/or a production. The name of the Author *must* appear on a separate line on which no other name appears, immediately following the title and *must* appear in size of type not less than fifty percent of the size of the title type.

ORIGINAL PRODUCTION CREDITS

◨ ST. JAMES THEATRE

A JUJAMCYN THEATRE

JAMES H. BINGER
CHAIRMAN

ROCCO LANDESMAN
PRESIDENT

PAUL LIBIN
PRODUCING DIRECTOR

JACK VIERTEL
CREATIVE DIRECTOR

Heidi Landesman

Rick Steiner, Frederic H. Mayerson, Elizabeth Williams,
Jujamcyn Theaters / TV ASAHI and Dodger Productions

present

Book and lyrics by
Marsha Norman

Music by
Lucy Simon

based on the novel by Frances Hodgson Burnett

with

(in alphabetical order)

John Babcock   Daisy Eagan   Alison Fraser
Rebecca Luker   John Cameron Mitchell   Mandy Patinkin
Barbara Rosenblat   Tom Toner   Robert Westenberg

Michael De Vries   Paul Jackel   Nancy Johnston
Rebecca Judd   Kimberly Mahon   Peter Marinos
Patricia Phillips   Peter Samuel   Drew Taylor   Kay Walbye

Teresa De Zarn   Frank Di Pasquale   Betsy Friday   Alec Timerman

Scenery by
Heidi Landesman

Costumes by
Theoni V. Aldredge

Lighting by
Tharon Musser

Orchestrations by
William D. Brohn

Musical Direction and
Vocal Arrangements
Michael Kosarin

Dance
Arrangements
Jeanine Levenson

Sound by
Otts Munderloh

Choreography by
Michael Lichtefeld

Casting
Wendy Ettinger

Production Stage Manager
Perry Cline

Musical Coordinator
John Miller

Hair and Makeup Design by
Robert DiNiro

General Management
David Strong Warner, Inc.

Production Manager
Peter Fulbright

Press Representation
Adrian Bryan-Brown

Directed by
Susan H. Schulman

Senior Associate Producer
Greg C. Mosher

Associate Producers

Rhoda Mayerson   Dentsu Inc. New York   Dorothy and Wendell Cherry
Margo Lion   126 Second Ave. Corp.   Playhouse Square Center

Originally produced by Virginia Stage Company, Charles Towers, Artistic Director.
The Producers and Theatre Management are members of The League of American Theaters and Producers, Inc.
The Producers wish to express their appreciation to Theatre Development Fund for its support of this production.

ORIGINAL BROADWAY CAST

LILY. . . . . Rebecca Luker
MARY LENNOX (Wed. Mats. and Thurs. Eves.) . . . . .Kimberly Mahon
IN COLONIAL INDIA, 1906:

FAKIR . . . . Peter Marinos
AYAH . . . . .Patricia Phillips
ROSE (MARY'S MOTHER) . . . . Kay Walbye
CAPTAIN ALBERT LENNOX. .Michael De Vries
LIEUTENANT PETER WRIGHT . . . . .Drew Taylor
LIEUTENANT IAN SHAW . . . . .Paul Jackel
MAJOR HOLMES. . . . . .Peter Samuel
CLAIRE (his wife) . . . . Rebecca Judd
ALICE (Rose's friend) . . . . Nancy Johnston
AT MISSELTHWAITE MANOR, NORTH YORKSHIRE, ENGLAND, 1906:

ARCHIBALD CRAVEN (Mary's uncle) . . . . .Mandy Patinkin
DR. NEVILLE CRAVEN (his brother). . . . . .Robert Westenberg
MRS. MEDLOCK (the housekeeper) . . . . Barbara Rosenblat
MARTHA (a chambermaid). . . . . .Alison Fraser
DICKON (her brother) .John Cameron Mitchell
BEN (the gardener) . . . . Tom Toner
COLIN. . . . . John Babcock
JANE. . . . . Teresa De Zarn
WILLIAM. . . . . Frank DiPasquale
BETSY . . . . .Betsy Friday
TIMOTHY . . . . .Alec Timerman
MRS. WINTHROP (the headmistress) . . . . Nancy Johnston

ALL OTHER PARTS ARE PLAYED BY THE ENSEMBLE

UNDERSTUDIES

Understudies never substitute for listed players unless a
specific announcement for the appearance is made at the time of
the performance.

Alternate for **MARY LENNOX** - Kimberly Mahon

Standby for **ARCHIBALD CRAVEN** - Greg Zirkle

For **LILY** - Teresa De Zarn, Nancy Johnston; For **MARY LENNOX** -
Melody Kay; For **ARCHIBALD CRAVEN** - Michael De Vries, Peter Samuel;
For **DR. NEVILLE CRAVEN** - Michael De Vries, Paul Jackel; For **MRS.
MEDLOCK** - Rebecca Judd, Jane Seaman; For **MARTHA** - Betsy Friday,
Jennifer Smith; For **DICKON** - Kevin Ligon, Alec Timerman; For **BEN**
- Bill Nolte, Drew Taylor; For **COLIN** - Joel E. Chaiken; For **ROSE**
- Teresa De Zarn, Betsy Friday; For **CAPTAIN ALBERT LENNOX** - Paul
Jackel, Greg Zerkle; For **FAKIR** - Kevin Ligon, Alec Timerman; For
AYAH - Rebecca Judd, Jennifer Smith; For **LIEUTENANT PETER WRIGHT**
- Frank DiPasquale, Bill Nolte; For **LIEUTENANT IAN SHAW** - Kevin
Ligon, Alec Timerman; For **MAJOR HOLMES** - Frank DiPasquale, Bill
Nolte; For **CLAIRE** - Betsy Friday, Jane Seaman; For **ALICE** - Betsy Friday,
Jennifer Smith; For **MRS. WINTHROP** - Rebecca Judd, Jennifer Smith.
Swings: Kevin Ugon, Bill Nolte, Jane Seaman, Jennifer Smith

CHARACTERS

MARY LENNOX – an orphan girl of about 10

COLIN CRAVEN – a sickly boy of about 10. Mary and Colin are cousins, their mothers were sisters

SPIRITS:

> **ALBERT** and **ROSE LENNOX** – Mary's Parents
>
> **LILY CRAVEN** – Colin's Mother

AT MISSELTHWAITE:

> **ARCHIBALD CRAVEN** – Mary's Uncle, Colin's Father
>
> **DR. NEVILLE CRAVEN** – Archibald's brother
>
> **MRS. MEDLOCK** – Archibald's housekeeper
>
> **BEN WEATHERSTAFF** – The Head Gardener
>
> **MARTHA** – a housemaid
>
> **DICKON** – Martha's brother, a magical boy who talks to birds
>
> **MRS. WINTHROP** – headmistress of the Aberdeen School for Girls
>
> Two **MEN** and Two **WOMEN** – servants, passengers, Indian officers, etc.

READERS: The chorus of the Spring version is comprised of any number of student singers of any age placed onstage at the discretion of the Director, not formally as if they were actually a chorus, but casually, as if they were reading the novel on the floor of their rooms. They are meant to observe and enjoy the scenes, sing as indicated, and watch the musical come to life before their eyes. They may also participate occasionally, as in the end of Act 1 and the Night Garden scene. The Director is free to make use of individuals who are gifted singers or dancers in scenes as appropriate. Our personal favorite idea is that the Readers are sometimes fellow travelers, sometimes garden sprites, and sometimes just readers. They need not always be reading, nor need they all appear in every scene. But we need at least one of them onstage in every scene to secure the convention. They are a chorus of choice for the Spring director. Our only request is that their presence never detract from the main action. The places where they must sing are indicated in the script and score. Some suggestions for their use will appear in the text.

PROLOGUE

(A brief prelude is heard.)

(Far downstage, seated by a dollhouse, we see a small girl, MARY LENNOX. She wears a nightdress. A READER may sit on the floor at some distance, leaning against the wall. The READER opens her copy of The Secret Garden *and LILY appears, as a spirit. LILY sings as the READER looks back down at her book.)*

LILY.

COME TO MY GARDEN,
NESTLED IN THE HILL.
THERE I'LL KEEP YOU SAFE BESIDE ME.

(LILY leaves the stage as an Indian flute plays. MARY LENNOX looks up, aware that something is wrong. She looks around and sees a snake.)

MARY. How strange and quiet it is. It sounds as if there is no one in this bungalow but me and that snake. Has everyone forgotten me?

(As the READER watches, MARY approaches the snake, singing and performing snake-charming hand movements taught to her by her Ayah.)

MARY.	*(PRONUNCIATION)*
A'O JADU KE, MAUSAM	*AH O, ZHAHDU KAY, MAU SUM*
A'O GARMIYO KE DIN.	*AH O, GARMEE YO, KAY DIN*
A'O MANTRA, TANTRA, YANTRA	*AH O MANTRA TANTRA YANTRA*
US KI BIMARI, HATA 'O	*OOS KEE BEEMAREE, AHTA O*

(Then suddenly we hear sounds and see behind MARY:)

7

(In India, the air is smoky from fires burning along the Ganges. Bodies wrapped in white muslin are carried by mourners. In the distance, ragas whine and drums pound, as the death bells proclaim the devastation of the cholera epidemic.)

*(An **OFFICER** comes into **MARY**'s room. He shouts back to someone.)*

OFFICER. Major! There's a girl in here.

MAJOR'S VOICE OFFSTAGE. Do you mean alive?

MARY. *(fiercely)* My name is Mary Lennox? Where is my Ayah? Why has no one come for me?

OFFICER. I'm afraid the cholera's taken everyone in the house, Miss. All British subjects were told to leave the city weeks ago. I don't know why your parents stayed.

MARY. They stayed because they were giving a silly party last night. But it was boring so I went to bed.

OFFICER. That's likely what saved you, Miss. According to the doctor, all the water was contaminated.

MARY. But where are my Mother and Father?

*(Two **SPIRITS** appear, **MARY**'s parents, **ALBERT** and **ROSE**. Their costumes should indicate they are spirits. Further, we should always be able to tell which woman spirit is **MARY**'s mother, Rose, and which is **COLIN**'s mother, Lily, when she appears. **LILY** is the blond one.)*

OFFICER. Your parents are dead, Miss. I'm so sorry.

MARY. But what will happen to me?

OFFICER. I'm told you have an Uncle, in England somewhere. He was married to your Mother's sister, Lily. She's dead, as well, I'm afraid.

MARY. I know that.

OFFICER. The Governor is trying to contact him now. Wait here.

*(The **OFFICER** leaves. **MARY** turns around to get something from her dresser.)*

*(**MARY**'s parents sing.)*

ROSE AND ALBERT AND READERS.
> THERE'S A GIRL WHOM NO ONE SEES
> THERE'S A GIRL WHO PLAYS ALONE
> THERE'S A GIRL WHO WAITS IN SILENCE FOR
> THE LIFE SHE'S NEVER KNOWN...
> FOR THE LIFE SHE'S NEVER KNOWN.
>
> *(As the* **OFFICER** *comes back for* **MARY,** *a library at Misselthwaite appears on the other side of the stage. The* **READER** *does not leave. She watches the next scene as well. The* **READERS** *help connect the scenes in this way.)*

The Library at Misselthwaite Manor

(MARY's uncle, **ARCHIBALD CRAVEN**, *confers with her* **UNCLE NEVILLE**, *a doctor, and* **MRS. MEDLOCK**, *the housekeeper.*)

DR. CRAVEN. Sorry to disturb you, Archie, but I have a letter from the Governor's Office in Bombay.

(scanning a telegram)

We regret to inform you that Captain Albert Lennox and his wife Rose have died of the cholera. All in the compound perished save your niece, Mary.

(looking up)

They're asking if they can send the girl here.

ARCHIBALD. This is no house for a child.

DR. CRAVEN. I couldn't agree more. But they found a will naming you as the girl's guardian. So we shall simply have to find a boarding school that will take her midterm.

MRS. MEDLOCK. There's a convent school not twenty mile away.

ARCHIBALD. And have my niece filling laundry tubs day and night? No. She will come here. It's what Lily would have wanted.

(At the mention of her name, **LILY**, *the ghost from the first moment, appears again.)*

DR. CRAVEN. But what will the girl have to do here, Archie? Do you want her wandering the halls?

MRS. MEDLOCK. We could engage a governess, sir, someone to watch her day and night.

ARCHIBALD. No. Let our young Mary come here to mourn her loss. And when she has recovered, then we will decide what is best for her.

(turning around)

And Mrs. Medlock, order the child some clothes. I won't have her dressed in black wandering around like a lost soul. That would make the house even sadder than it is.

MRS. MEDLOCK. Yes sir.

(**ARCHIE** *and* **DR. CRAVEN** *exit.*)

(*A train platform appears, with* **MARY** *and the* **OFFI-CER** *from India standing beside a huge stack of luggage.* **MARY** *is wearing all black. Several* **READERS** *may sit on train platforms.*)

MARY. I don't like it here. It's too cold.

(**MRS. MEDLOCK** *approaches the* **OFFICER**.)

MRS. MEDLOCK. Good evening, Major. I'm Mrs. Medlock, Mr. Craven's housekeeper. Is this the girl?

MAJOR. Yes ma'am. And here's her papers and the death certificates.

(**MRS. MEDLOCK** *accepts the girl and the papers, with little enthusiasm.*)

MRS. MEDLOCK. Thank you, Major.

(*A train sound is heard.* **MRS. MEDLOCK** *and* **MARY** *take their seats on something that indicates their compartment on a train. Music begins.*)

MRS. MEDLOCK. Well, now. I suppose you'd like to know something about where you're going.

MARY. Would I?

MRS. MEDLOCK. But don't you care about your new home?

MARY. It doesn't matter whether I care or not.

MRS. MEDLOCK. Well you're right not to care. Why you're being brought to Misselthwaite I'll never know.

MARY. That's an ugly name.

(**MARY***'s mother and father, as* **SPIRITS***, travel with them. They sing, with the* **READERS** *who are dressed as passengers, or are looking up from their books.*)

ROSE, ALBERT, AND READERS.

> HIGH ON A HILL SITS A BIG OLD HOUSE
> WITH SOMETHING WRONG INSIDE IT.
> SPIRITS HAUNT THE HALLS AND
> MAKE NO EFFORT NOW, TO HIDE IT.
>
> WHAT WILL PUT THEIR SOULS TO REST
> AND STOP THEIR CEASELESS SIGHING.
> WHY DO THEY CALL OUT CHILDREN'S NAMES
> AND SPEAK OF ONE WHO'S DYING.

MRS. MEDLOCK. Misselthwaite is your Uncle Archie's estate. But he isn't going to trouble himself about you, that's sure and certain. He never troubles himself about anyone.

> (**MARY** *isn't listening.*)

ROSE, ALBERT AND READERS.

> AND THE MASTER HEARS THE WHISPERS
> ON THE STAIRWAYS DARK AND STILL.
> AND THE SPIRITS KNOW THE SECRETS
> OF THE HOUSE UPON THE HILL.

MRS. MEDLOCK. He's a hunchback, you see. And a sour young man he was, and got no good of all his money and big place 'til he were married.

> (*a moment*)

To your mother's sister, Lily. She was a sweet, pretty thing and he'd have walked the world over to get her a blade of grass that she wanted. Nobody thought she'd marry him, but marry him she did, and it wasn't for his money either. But then when she died…

MARY. How did she die?

MRS. MEDLOCK. It made him worse than ever. He hardly speaks at all now, and when he does it's only to talk to ghosts and wander the hallways.

> (*a moment*)

He travels most of the time now. It's his brother, Dr. Craven, who makes all the decisions these days.

ROSE, ALBERT AND READERS.

> HIGH ON A HILL
> SITS A BIG OLD HOUSE
> WITH SOMETHING WRONG INSIDE IT.
> SOMEONE'S DIED AND SOMEONE'S LEFT
> ALONE AND CAN'T ABIDE IT.
>
> THERE IN THE HOUSE LIVES A LONELY MAN
> STILL HAUNTED BY HER BEAUTY,
> ASKING WHAT A LIFE CAN BE
> WHERE NAUGHT REMAINS BUT DUTY.

> (**MARY** *looks out the window.*)

MARY. Is it always so ugly here?

MRS. MEDLOCK. It's the moor, it is. Miles and miles of wild land that nothing grows on but heather and gorse and broom, and nothing lives on but wild ponies and sheep.

MARY. What is that awful howling sound?

MRS. MEDLOCK. That's the wind, blowing through the bushes. They call it wuthering, that sound. But look there, that tiny light far across there. That'll be the gate it will.

ROSE, ALBERT, AND READERS.

> AND THE MASTER HEARS THE WHISPERS
> ON THE STAIRWAY DARK AND STILL.
> AND THE SPIRITS KNOW THE SECRETS
> OF THE HOUSE UPON THE HILL.

At Misselthwaite

(**MARY** *and* **MRS. MEDLOCK** *are met by* **DR. CRAVEN**.)

(*Off to one side, the spirits of* **ALBERT** *and* **ROSE**, *come to stand by the spirit of* **LILY**. *They greet each other. The bond between these three will be important to us here.*)

MRS. MEDLOCK. Mary Lennox, this is Dr. Craven, your Uncle's brother.

DR. CRAVEN. You're to take her to her room. Her Uncle Archibald doesn't want to see her.

MRS. MEDLOCK. Very good, Doctor.

(**MRS. MEDLOCK** *takes* **MARY** *upstairs*.)

ROSE, ALBERT, AND LILY.
THERE'S A GIRL WHOM NO ONE SEES.
THERE'S A GIRL WHO LIVES ALONE.
THERE'S A GIRL WHO PRAYS IN SILENCE FOR
THE LIFE SHE'S NEVER KNOWN.

READERS.
FOR THE LIFE SHE'S NEVER KNOWN
FOR THE LIFE SHE'S NEVER KNOWN

In Mary's Room

(**MRS. MEDLOCK** *shows* **MARY** *into her room.*)

MRS. MEDLOCK. Well, here you are. This room and the next are where you'll live. But you mustn't expect there to be people to play with you. You'll have to look after yourself. But when you're in the house, don't go wandering about. Your uncle won't have it.

(**MARY** *walks across to the window.*)

MARY. Won't have it.

(*Finally,* **MRS. MEDLOCK** *turns out the light and shuts* **MARY**'s *door hard. The sound echoes through the halls.*)

MRS. MEDLOCK. Good night, then.

(**MARY** *gets in her bed, and pulls up the covers. The spirits are seen in dim light. Quietly, they sing the song* **MARY** *sang to the snake. She sits up sometime during the song, and sings the last part with them.*)

ALBERT, ROSE, AND LILY.
A'O JADU KE, MAUSAM
A'O GARMIYO KE DIN.
A'O MANTRA TANTRA YANTRA
US KI BIMARI, (**MARY** *joins in the chant*) HATA 'O

(**MARY** *settles back down to sleep, but then she hears a cry from somewhere in the house. It startles the* **READERS** *too.*)

MARY. What was that?

(*She hears the crying again.*)

MARY. It's someone crying.

(*In her exhaustion, she falls back on the bed at last. Piano transition to next scene.*)

Scene One
Mary's Sitting Room – Morning

(**MARTHA**, *a sturdy, curious Yorkshire girl, enters* **MARY***'s sitting room humming a melody to herself.* **READERS** *should be very still during this scene.*)

MARTHA.

SKIP, SKIPPED THE LADIES
TO THE MASTER'S GATE.
SIP, SIPPED THE LADIES
WHILE THE MASTER ATE.
TIP-TOED THE CHAMBERMAID
AND STOLE THEIR PEARLS.
SNIP, SNIP THE GARDENER
AND CUT OFF THEIR CURLS...

(**MARY** *wakes with a start. She is frightened and furious.*)

MARY. Who are you? Are you my servant?

MARTHA. Me name is Martha. And now tha'rt up, I'll make tha' bed.

MARY. Aren't you going to dress me first? In India, my Ayah dressed me.

MARTHA. Well then, it'll do tha' good to wait on thysel' a bit. Tis fair a wonder grand folks children...

MARY. What is this language you speak?

MARTHA. Well of course you've not heard any Yorkshire, livin' in India, have ye. But you'll get used to it. Why I didn't know what to expect from you either, lassie. When I heard you was comin', I thought you'd be a solid brown, I did.

MARY. Stop looking at me!

(**MARTHA** *tries to comfort her.*)

MARTHA. Don't cry now, lassie, I didn't know you'd be so easy vexed. You're not brown at all. More yellow, I'd say.

MARY. *(furious)* I'm not crying! Leave me alone!

MARTHA. I beg your pardon, miss. I'll help you on with your clothes if you like –

MARY. These are not my clothes!

MARTHA. Aye, Miss. Your Uncle ordered them for you from London. Now let's get these new things on and wrap you up warm so you can run out and play. That'll give you stomach for your porridge.

MARY. I don't want to go out! Mrs. Medlock said there's nothing out there but a big old park.

(**MARTHA** *begins helping* **MARY** *with the clothes, but it is a struggle.*)

MARY. Maybe you'll run into my brother Dickon out there.

MARY. Does he work here too?

MARTHA. If somethin' is sick, he takes a look at it, sure he does. And finds the ponies that run off, and the eggs that roll out of the nests.

MARY. *(pointing out the window)* What is that?

MARTHA. That's the moor it is, like a dull purple sea this morning. Do you like it?

MARY. I hate it.

MARTHA. Well, of course you do because now it looks so big and bare. But in the spring, the moor is fair covered in gorse and heather, and there's such a lot of fresh air. My brother Dickon –

(**MARTHA** *holds up a dress out for* **MARY** *to put on.*)

MARY. Stop talking about Dickon. I don't like boys.

MARTHA. I don't like him sometimes myself, but he's got a pony that wakes him up, and birds and sheep and such as eats right out of his hand. Now don't tell me you don't like ponies.

MARY. *(still very put out)* Very well then. When I am dressed, you may take me out to meet your brother.

MARTHA. Oh I can't do that, Miss. I work inside, not outside.

MARY. You are my servant! You'll do as I say!

(**MARTHA** *hears* **MRS. MEDLOCK**'s *bell.*)

MARTHA. I can't, Miss. That's Mrs. Medlock's bell. You'll have to find your way out yourself. It's down the stairs, past the ballroom.....

MARY. I'll find it.

MARTHA. Once you're outside, ye'll stay to the left and come to the gardens. But be wary of Ben, the gardener, he's none too friendly. And there's one garden that's locked up. So you'll stay away from that as well.

MARY. Why would you lock up a garden?

MARTHA. *(hearing the bell)* I must run. And I brought you a skipping rope.

(giving her the skip rope)

Goodbye, Mary.

MARY. Goodbye.

(**MARY** *tries a few jumps of the rope, and tries to remember the words to the song.*)

SKIP SKIPPED THE LADIES TO THE...TO THE MONSTER'S GATE...

SLIP SLIPPED THE LADIES WHILE THE MONSTER ATE....

(She throws the rope down in despair, walks away, then walks back and picks it up.)

TRIP TRIPPED THE FRAIDIES TO THE...

I can't do it. I can't.

(But she takes the rope with her as she runs out of the house.)

Outside the House

(**MARY** *walks toward the gardens.*)

MARY. (*She calls out.*) Dickon? Is anybody here?

(*Music begins and the bushes and walls of the garden turn, revealing* **BEN WEATHERSTAFF**, *the stooped but spry Head Gardener.* **MARY** *wanders the gardens as* **BEN** *sings.* **READERS** *may sit on garden walls.*)

BEN.

PLANT A HEDGE, CUT IT BACK
DIG A HOLE, TRY TO FILL IT,
PLANT A ROSE, TIE IT BACK
FIND A MOLE, TRY TO KILL IT.

IT'S A MAZE THIS MORNING,
IT'S A MAZE OF WAYS,
ANY MAN CAN SPEND HIS DAY.
IT'S A MAZE THIS GARDEN,
IT'S A MAZE OF PATHS,
BUT A SOUL CAN FIND THE WAY.

BUT AN OLD MAN KNOWS HOW A YEAR IT GOES.
HOW THE COLD HARD GROUND
IN THE SPRING COMES ROUND.
HOW THE SEEDS TAKE HOLD,
HOW THE FERNS UNFOLD,
HOW AN ENGLISH GARDEN GROWS.)

(**MARY** *is very frustrated. She calls out.*)

MARY. Dickon, where are you?

(*She comes round a hedge and is startled to see* **BEN** *talking to a Robin.*)

BEN. Aye now, Robin. That'll be the little wench from India.

MARY. Are you talking to a *bird*?

BEN. This Robin is no ordinary bird. He's the only friend I've got.

MARY. Well I have no friends at all. People don't like me and I've never played with anyone.

BEN. Tha' and me are a good bit alike. We're neither of us good looking, and we're both of us as sour as we look.

(She stomps off and **BEN** *goes back to work, singing.)*

MISS A STEP, TRIP AND FALL.
MISS THE PATH, MEET THE WALL.
MISS THE WAY, MISS A TURN.
GETTING LOST IS HOW YOU LEARN.

IT'S A MAZE, THIS GARDEN,
IT'S A MAZE OF PATHS
MEANT TO LEAD A MAN ASTRAY.
TURNING LEFT AND THEN
TURNING LEFT AGAIN'S
HOW A SOUL CAN FIND THE WAY.

BUT AN OLD MAN KNOWS HOW A YEAR IT GOES.
HOW THE COLD HARD GROUND
IN THE SPRING COMES ROUND.
HOW THE ROSES BLOOM,
IF THEY HAVE THE ROOM,
HOW AN ENGLISH GARDEN GROWS.

READERS.

TURNING LEFT TURNING LEFT
TURNING LEFT AGAIN.
TURNING LEFT TURNING LEFT
TURNING LEFT AND THEN
ROUND, ROUND THE OLD SUN GOES
AND AN ENGLISH GARDEN GROWS

A Few Days Later

*(**MARY** skips into sight. She's getting better at skipping rope. She follows the sound of the Robin. **BEN** sees her.)*

BEN. Back again today, are ye?

*(**BEN** continues working as **MARY** looks around. **LILY** enters when she is mentioned.)*

MARY. I know where the Robin lives. It's that locked up garden. Am I right? What's in that garden?

BEN. That was Miss Lily's garden. When she died, Mr. Archibald said nobody was to go in there ever again. And he locked the door and buried the key.

MARY. But where is the door?

BEN. Can't say, Missy. Over the years, the ivy's grown up so thick, even I don't know where it is anymore.

MARY. But aren't you worried that Aunt Lily's garden is all dead with nobody taking care of it? Maybe the real reason the Robin is chirping at you is he wants you to climb over his garden wall and work on it.

BEN. Maybe he is, but I can't go losin' my job on the advice of a bird, now can I. Now you go off and play with Dickon. I have work to do.

*(**MARY** hears the sound of the Robin. The **READERS** hear it too and turn toward the sound.)*

MARY. I haven't found Dickon yet, and I've been looking everywhere!

*(**MARTHA** appears suddenly, and takes **MARY**'s hand.)*

MARTHA. Well now, Mary. Ye've spent another whole day in the garden ye didn't want to go to. It's time for your dinner.

MARY. I don't want any dinner. I can't sleep in that house. There's someone crying every night. Is there a ghost here?

MARTHA. You're not afraid of ghosts, are ye?

MARY. If he starts crying again tonight, I'm going to kill him, whether he's a ghost or not.

BEN.

FOR AN OLD MAN KNOWS, HOW A YEAR IT GOES,

HOW THE COLD HARD GROUND

IN THE SPRING COMES ROUND.

HOW IN TIME IT SHOWS

HOW A GARDEN GROWS

HOW AN ENGLISH GARDEN GROWS.

*(***MARY*** leaves ***MARTHA*** standing there.)*

Scene Two
In the Ballroom – Night

*(**UNCLE ARCHIE** sits in his chair. He seems lost in memory. He studies a large portrait of **LILY**. He sings. A reader reads but does not look up 'til **MARY** comes in.)*

ARCHIBALD.

A GIRL I SAW IN A VALLEY,
A GIRL I HARDLY KNEW,
A GIRL AT WORK IN A GARDEN
GREW TO LOVE ME.

*(**LILY** steps out of the portrait and approaches him.)*

LILY.

A MAN WHO CAME TO MY VALLEY,
A MAN I HARDLY KNEW,
A MAN WHO CAME TO MY GARDEN
GREW TO LOVE ME.

FROM THE GATE,
HE CALLED OUT SO KINDLY,
"LASS WOULDST THOU 'LOW ME
REST HERE, I'VE RIDDEN QUITE FAR."

(The music seems to draw them together.)

ARCHIBALD.

"SHARE MY TEA," SHE
BADE ME SO GENTLY
OATCAKES AND CREAM,
SWEET PLUMS IN A JAR...

LILY.

THEN EVERY DAY TO MY GARDEN,
THIS MAN, WHO MIGHT HE BE,
CAME BEARING BASKETS OF ROSES,
FOR HE LOVED ME.

ARCHIBALD.

ALL I OWN, I'D GIVE

LILY.

...JUST A GARDEN...

ARCHIBALD.
ALL I WOULD ASK IS NEVER TO
LILY.
...NEVER TO LEAVE;
ARCHIBALD.
SAY YOU'LL HAVE ME,
LILY.
SAFE WILL YOU KEEP ME,
LILY AND ARCHIBALD.
WHERE YOU WOULD LEAD ME,
THERE I WOULD, THERE I WOULD
THERE I WOULD GO.....

(Finally, they embrace, begin to dance, and sing in a little round.)

LILY.	**ARCHIBALD.**
A MAN WHO CAME TO MY VALLEY	A GIRL WHO CAME TO MY VALLEY
A MAN I HARDLY KNEW	A GIRL I HARDLY KNEW
A MAN WHO GAVE ME A GARDEN	A GIRL WHO GAVE ME A GARDEN
GREW TO LOVE ME.	GREW TO LOVE ME

(They are so happy, so deeply in love. They dance.)

*(**MARY** enters the Ballroom, sees a man dancing by himself and coughs. The music stops. **LILY** exits. The **READER** looks up.)*

ARCHIBALD. Who's there?

MARY. *(stepping out of the shadows)* It's Mary Lennox, sir. Are you my Uncle Archibald?

ARCHIBALD. *(trying to regain his composure)* Yes, I am. Good evening, child.

MARY. Are you going to be my father now?

ARCHIBALD. I am your guardian. Though I am a poor one for any child. Your mother and my wife were sisters, as I'm sure you know.

MARY. Is my Aunt Lily a ghost now? I heard someone crying in the house again tonight. But I don't know anything about ghosts. Is my father a ghost now? Does everyone who dies become a ghost?

ARCHIBALD. They're only a ghost if someone alive is still holding onto them.

MARY. Maybe what I heard was mother, telling me to be nice so you'll keep me.

ARCHIBALD. The house is haunted, child, day and night. But it is yours to live in as long as I am master here. I offer you my deepest sympathies on your arrival.

(He walks over toward the portrait, seeming to forget her. After a moment –)

MARY. Did my mother have any other family?

*(As **MARY** turns around, **MRS.MEDLOCK** appears.)*

MRS. MEDLOCK. Mary Lennox, what are you doing out of bed?

MARY. I heard someone crying.

MRS. MEDLOCK. That were the wind.

MARY. That were not the wind.

MRS. MEDLOCK. That *were* the wind, and it'll get a lot worse before it's through. Come on.

Scene Three
In the Garden

(Wandering on another day. **MARY** *is getting better at skipping rope.)*

MARY.

SKIP SKIPPED THE LADIES TO THE MASTER'S GATE.
SIP SIPPED THE LADIES WHILE THE MASTER ATE.
TIP-TOED THE CHAMBER MAID AND STOLE THEIR PEARLS.
SNIP, SNIPPED THE GARDENER AND CUT OFF THEIR CURLS.

(Suddenly, **MARY** *comes upon* **DICKON**. **READERS** *watch.)*

DICKON. Eh up. Hello there.

MARY. *(as if she doesn't know)* Who are you?

DICKON. I'm Martha's brother, Dickon.

MARY. But why haven't I seen you before?

DICKON. A body has to walk gentle and speak low when wild things are about.

(then quickly)

But look here. Me mother's sent you a penny's worth of seeds for your garden. There's columbine and poppies by the handful.

(A Robin whistle is heard. **MARY** *moves away from him.)*

MARY. I don't have a garden.

DICKON. But don't you want one? One of your own, I mean.

(The Robin is heard again.)

MARY. I want to go in that garden. Where the Robin lives.

(The Robin whistles again. **DICKON** *takes* **MARY**'s *skipping rope and plays with it.)*

Have you ever been in that garden?

(The Robin chirps again and flies to another side of the wall. They follow the Robin.)

DICKON. It's not mine to go into, Mary. But it might be yours, I can't say. He's been keepin' it safe for somebody, that much I know.

MARY. He has?

DICKON. Same way as the ivy grown up to hide the door. But maybe the Robin is waitin' to hear why you want to go in there, exactly. Go on now. I'll translate into Yorkshire for ye 'til ye get the way of it.

(And there is a trill from the Robin.)

MARY.

I...

DICKON.

SHE...

MARY.

I'M A GIRL...

DICKON.

SHE IS A LASS
AS TOOK A GRAIDLEY FANCY TO THEE
DOST THA' FEAR?

MARY.

THA' MUN NOT FEAR,

DICKON.

SHE'S TOOK THEE ON
FOR LIKE TO VEX THEE.
NOWT O' THE SORT,

MARY.

NOWT O' THE SORT,

DICKON.

SHE KNOWS FAIR WELL
SHE MUN NOT FRIGHT THEE.

MARY.

CANNA THA' SHOW ME,

DICKON.

FAIR WELL DOST THA' KNOW HER,

MARY.

SHOW ME THA' KEY.

DICKON.

SHOW HER THA' KEY.

(The Robin chirps.)

MARY. What did he say?

DICKON. He said you still didn't tell him *why* you want to see his garden.

(*The* **READERS** *watch her as she considers this question.*)

MARY.

I NEED A PLACE WHERE I CAN GO,
WHERE I CAN WHISPER WHAT I KNOW,
WHERE I CAN WHISPER WHO I LIKE
AND WHERE I GO TO SEE THEM.

I NEED A PLACE WHERE I CAN HIDE,
WHERE NO ONE SEES MY LIFE INSIDE,
WHERE I CAN MAKE MY PLANS
AND WRITE THEM DOWN
SO I CAN READ THEM.

A PLACE WHERE I CAN BID MY HEART BE STILL
AND IT WILL MIND ME.
A PLACE WHERE I CAN GO WHEN I AM LOST,
AND THERE I'LL FIND ME.

I NEED A PLACE TO SPEND THE DAY,
WHERE NO ONE SAYS TO GO OR STAY,
WHERE I CAN TAKE MY PEN AND DRAW
THE GIRL I MEAN TO BE.....
THE GIRL I MEAN TO BE.

DICKON. It's a good place, this garden.

(*The Robin trills again, and* **MARY**'s *attention is drawn back to him.*)

MARY. Does he like me? Can you tell?

DICKON. That he does. Well, then. I'm off.

MARY. But where are you going?

DICKON. I can't say. But I'll see you tomorrow sure enough. And if you need me before then, well, now that you and the Robin is talking, he always knows where I am.

MARY. All right, then. Bye.

(**MARY** *walks off a little way, then remembers her skipping rope. She notices the Robin is pecking at something.* **LILY** *appears.*)

MARY. *(cont.)* Now what are you doing down there? You won't find anything for your nest buried in the ground.

(Then she hears a metallic clink, and hears the Robin chirp even harder.)

What do you have there? May I see? Maybe I can help

(She bends over, brushes away the leaves and sees....)

But what is this? It's something metal.

(looking at it)

It's a key!

(She jumps up, and once again we hear the Robin.)

It's the key to the garden!

(a moment)

It was right here all along! Dickon! Come see!

(She stands holding the key close, then hears:)

(A HUGE SOUND OF THUNDER)

MRS. MEDLOCK. Mary Lennox!

(She puts the key in her pocket quickly and runs toward the house.)

MARY. Coming!

(turning back to the Robin)

Oh thank you. Thank you so much.

(MARTHA and MRS. MEDLOCK stand at the door to the house, looking out at the approaching bad weather.)

MRS. MEDLOCK. Mr. Archibald wants to see Mary in his library. You must get her ready at once. And see that her hair is combed...

MARTHA. Yes, Mum.

MRS. MEDLOCK. ...and change her dress.

Scene Four
Archibald's Library

(DR. CRAVEN presents ARCHIE with some papers to sign.)

DR. CRAVEN. I heard you wandering the hallways again last night, Archie. Would you like me to give you something to help you sleep?

(ARCHIE does not want to sign papers or talk or anything, it seems.)

ARCHIBALD. Father should've given Misselthwaite to you, Neville, not me. I hate coming here.

DR. CRAVEN. You needn't feel like such a prisoner, Archie. There is no reason why you simply couldn't return to Paris.

ARCHIBALD. I can't leave my son alone here, Neville. You know that.

DR. CRAVEN. But what good does it do to sit by the boy's bed, night after night, hoping for a miracle.

(MARY enters.)

MARY. You sent for me, sir?

ARCHIBALD. Yes, child. Come in. Perhaps we can manage to have a moment before the storm carries us away. Take a chair.

(She takes a seat. DR. CRAVEN backs away.)

MARY. Thank you, sir.

(ARCHIE has no idea what to say to her. Finally –)

ARCHIBALD. Are you well? Do they take good care of you?

MARY. Yes, sir. Thank you, sir.

ARCHIBALD. I'm sorry it's been so long since we've spoken. It's just I keep forgetting you.

(another pause)

I intended to find you a school to go to or…

MARY. Oh no. Please don't send me away!

ARCHIBALD. No, of course not.

(then quickly)

But perhaps you would enjoy a governess.

MARY. Please don't make me have a governess, sir. There are so many gardens to walk around in, and so much to learn about them. Martha's teaching me to skip, and Dickon –

ARCHIBALD. Play outside, then, if you like, but is there anything you need? Would you like some toys, or books or dolls perhaps?

MARY. Might I have a bit of earth, sir?

ARCHIBALD. Earth?

MARY. To plant seeds in, yes sir. A garden.

*(**ARCHIE** is clearly moved by this request. **DR. CRAVEN** is disturbed.)*

I didn't know about them in India. I was always ill and tired and it was too hot. But here, I might have a real garden if you would allow it, sir.

ARCHIBALD. All right, then. You may have your earth. Take as much earth as you want.

MARY. Thank you very much, sir.

*(**MARY** leaves the room. **DR. CRAVEN** realizes **ARCHIE** seems even more despondent than before.)*

DR. CRAVEN. What is it, Archie?

ARCHIBALD. It's much worse being back this time. The dreams are much more vivid. And I hear things. Voices in the hall, and footsteps.

DR. CRAVEN. It's the girl, Archie. She reminds you of Lily.

ARCHIBALD. Of Lily?

DR. CRAVEN. I see the resemblance myself. Though your wife's hair was more golden, the girl has Lily's eyes. We need to send her away.

ARCHIBALD. But you can see she's lonely, Neville. I should have more conversations with her.

DR. CRAVEN. I don't think that is wise, Archie. Until you are ready to send Mary to a school, it is my professional advice that you continue to avoid her. And now if I may have your signature on these leases.

(And with a crash of thunder and a stroke of lightning, the storm hits.)

Scene Five
Hallways of Misselthwaite

(**MRS. MEDLOCK** *directs the servants to prepare for the storm.* **READERS** *may help with the preparations.*)

MRS. MEDLOCK. The storm is upon us. We'll need all the shutters closed and all the doors shut. No one is to go outside, no lamps lighted except the ones in your hands.

(**MARY** *hears the crying again. She walks out of her room, irritated and terrified.*)

MARY. Martha!

MARTHA. It's all right Mary. It's just the storm.

MARY. It wasn't the storm. I heard someone crying.

MARTHA. No, child.

MARY. And this isn't the first time either.

MRS. MEDLOCK. Martha! We need you out here!

MARY. There is someone crying in this house, and I'm going to find out who it is.

MARTHA. You stay here in your room. They don't want you wandering about.

(**MRS. MEDLOCK** *calls from the hall.*)

MRS. MEDLOCK. Martha!

(**MARTHA** *leaves the room and* **MARY** *sneaks out into the hall.* **MARY** *sings, over the wind and the sounds of the storm.*)

LILY.

OO——

MARY.

I HEARD SOMEONE CRYING,
WHO THO' COULD IT BE?
SOMEONE IN THIS HOUSE
WHOM NO ONE SEEMS TO SEE,
SOMEONE NO ONE SEEMS TO
HEAR EXCEPT FOR ME,
I HEARD SOMEONE CRYING
MAYBE IT WAS ME.

READERS.
> MAYBE IT WAS SOMEONE WHO IS FRIGHTENED HERE, A LOT
> LIKE ME
> MAYBE IT WAS SOMEONE WHO IS SCARED OF LIGHTNING,
> JUST LIKE——

In the Ballroom

(DR. CRAVEN comes in the ballroom, quite alarmed by the state of the weather.)

DR. CRAVEN. Archie, there's a storm coming.

(Undisturbed by the storm, ARCHIE stands and looks at the portrait of LILY.)

LILY.

OO——

(NEVILLE leaves the room, giving up on getting any help from ARCHIE.)

ARCHIBALD.

I HEARD SOMEONE SINGING.
WHO THOUGH COULD IT BE?
MAYBE IT WAS LILY CALLING OUT TO ME.
MAYBE SHE'S NOT GONE
SO FAR AWAY AS I'VE BEEN TOLD.
I HEARD SOMEONE SINGING,
MAYBE IT WAS SHE.

In the Upstairs Hall

(MARTHA runs into MARY in the hallway.)

MARTHA. Mary, get back in your room.

(But MARY eludes her and continues to sing and search for the source of the crying.)

(ARCHIE has come out into the hallway now too. This whole section should be people rushing around in a maze of hallways carrying candles and trying to get their jobs done. Because they're all so preoccupied, MARY manages to avoid being seen, as she searches for the source of the crying. READERS are present in this section.)

MARY.

MAYBE IT WAS SOMEONE HERE WHO CANNOT SLEEP,
A LOT LIKE ME

MARTHA.

MAYBE IT WAS SOMEONE WHO IS SCARED OF THUNDER,
JUST LIKE ME

(MARTHA exits down a hall. LILY appears on a stair, or perhaps quite near ARCHIE.)

LILY.

I HEARD SOMEONE CRYING,
THOUGH I CAN'T SAY WHO.
SOMEONE IN THIS HOUSE
WITH NOTHING LEFT TO DO.
SOUNDED LIKE A FATHER
LEFT ALONE HIS LOVE GROWN COLD
I HEARD SOMEONE CRYING
MAYBE IT WAS YOU.

READERS.

MAYBE I WAS DREAMING OF A GARDEN GROWING FAR
BELOW,
MAYBE I WAS DREAMING OF A LIFE THAT I WILL NEVER
KNOW.

(There is another enormous bolt of lightning. All three are singing, the wind is wuthering, and the crying is getting worse.)

MARY, LILY, AND ARCHIBALD.

I HEARD SOMEONE CALLING,
WHO THOUGH COULD IT BE.
SOMEONE IN THIS HOUSE
WHOM NO ONE SEEMS TO SEE.
SOMEONE NO ONE SEEMS TO HEAR
EXCEPT FOR ME.
I HEARD SOMEONE CRYING,
MAYBE IT WAS ME.

LILY.

OO——

(Suddenly, **MARY** *comes upon a door and opens it. A ghostly form on the bed screams at her.)*

Scene Six
Colin's Room

COLIN. Get out!

*(**MARY** gasps, then steps closer.)*

MARY. Who are you?

COLIN. Who are *you?* Are you a ghost?

MARY. No I am not. I am Mary Lennox. Archibald Craven is my uncle.

COLIN. How do I know you're not a ghost?

MARY. I'll pinch you if you like. That will show you how real I am. Who are you?

COLIN. I am Colin. Archibald Craven is my father. I see no one and no one sees me. I am going to die.

*(**MARY** takes this very seriously.)*

MARY. How do you know?

COLIN. Because I hear everybody whispering about it, that's how. If I live, I may be a hunchback, but I shan't live.

(And now she dismisses it.)

MARY. Well, I've seen lots of dead people, and you don't look like any of them.

COLIN. Dead people! Where did you come from?

MARY. From India. My parents died there of the cholera. I was sent here because my mother and your mother were sisters. But they didn't tell me about you.

COLIN. That's because they hate me. Because my mother was beautiful and she died when I was born. My father won't even come see me when I'm awake. Sometimes at night he comes to read to me, but I pretend to be asleep.

*(**MARY** wishes she hadn't said anything about the garden.)*

MARY. Do you mean you have always been in this bed?

COLIN. Sometimes I go to the seaside, but I won't stay because people stare at me.

MARY. If you don't like people to see you, do you want me to go away?

COLIN. I want you to come back first thing tomorrow morning and tell me all about India. In the books my father sends me, I've read that elephants can swim. Have you ever seen them swim? They seem too altogether large to be swimmers, unless maybe they use their ears to…

MARY. But I can't come and talk to you in the morning. I have to go outside. I found something and I want to show it to Dickon.

COLIN. Who's Dickon?

MARY. He's Martha's brother. He's my friend.

(Suddenly, COLIN*'s despotic temperament flares.)*

COLIN. If you go outside with that Dickon instead of coming here to talk to me, I'll send him away.

*(*MARY *is outraged.)*

MARY. You can't send Dickon away!

COLIN. I can do whatever I want. If I live, this entire place will belong to me someday. And they all know that.

MARY. You little Rajah! If you send Dickon away, I'll never come into this room again!

COLIN. I'll make you. They'll drag you in here!

MARY. I won't even look at you. I'll stare at the floor!

COLIN. You are a selfish thing.

MARY. You're more selfish than I am. You're the most selfish boy I ever saw.

COLIN. I'm selfish because I'm dying!

MARY. You just say that to make people feel sorry for you. If you were a nice boy it might be true, but you're too nasty to die!

(She turns and stomps away toward the door.)

(Suddenly, there is another terrible clap of thunder, the door opens and MRS. MEDLOCK *and* DR. CRAVEN *rush in. They are horrified. As* DR. CRAVEN *goes to the boy,* MRS. MEDLOCK *grabs* MARY.*)*

MRS. MEDLOCK. Mary Lennox! Get away from him!

(MRS. MEDLOCK pulls MARY away from the bed as DR. CRAVEN opens his bag.)

DR. CRAVEN. *(preparing the injection)* I was afraid of something like this.

MRS. MEDLOCK. *(to MARY)* The one rule you were given you have violated!

MARY. But I've never seen him before!

DR. CRAVEN. How can I hope to succeed with him if my orders are not followed?

MRS. MEDLOCK. I've told her to stay in her room, but she refuses to obey.

COLIN. Get away from me!

(As DR. CRAVEN wrestles with COLIN, MRS. MEDLOCK takes MARY firmly in hand and walks her to the door.)

MRS. MEDLOCK. Do you see what you've done?

(The Indian drum begins.)

MARY. Why didn't you tell me he was here?

(DR. CRAVEN gives the boy a shot.)

MRS. MEDLOCK. He is not well. He could die from something like this!

MARY. No!

MRS. MEDLOCK. Now go to your room!

MARY. I'm going outside.

MRS. MEDLOCK. No!

MARY. You don't want me. Nobody wants me!

MRS. MEDLOCK. Get out!

COLIN. Mary!!!!!!!!!

(There is another violent stroke of lightning and MRS. MEDLOCK pushes MARY out the door and she runs down the stairs and outside)

Scene Seven
Outside In the Storm

*(The sounds of the storm explode now, and **A'O JADU KE** repeats with a new urgency. There are drums and wailing. **MARY** is wearing the same nightdress she had on in the beginning. **READERS** may appear as wanderers, or may gather as a group, reading.)*

MARY. Mother! Father! I want to go home!

*(**MARY** runs wildly, trying to find anyone to help, anything she can do. But the faster she runs, the more terrified she becomes.)*

Mother! Mother!

*(In the storm, **MARY** finds her mother, only to have her torn away by the storm. **MARY** whirls around.)*

Father! Where are you? Father?

(He's looking for her too, though too sick to really see her.)

ALBERT. Mary! Mary!

*(Finally, **MARY** finds her father and clings to him, but he is torn away from her and carried away. She stands, frozen still, as in the opening scene, wearing the white nightdress. And then **LILY** appears upstage.)*

LILY.

COME TO MY GARDEN,
NESTLED IN THE HILL.
THERE I'LL KEEP YOU SAFE BESIDE ME.
COME TO MY GARDEN,
REST THERE IN MY ARMS.
THERE I'LL SEE YOU SAFELY GROWN AND
ON YOUR WAY.

STAY THERE IN MY GARDEN,
WHERE LOVE GROWS FREE AND WILD.
COME TO MY GARDEN,
COME SWEET CHILD.

(**MARY** *turns and sees* **LILY***'s open arms.*)

(**MARY** *walks toward her, and* **LILY** *leads* **MARY** *to the garden wall, pulls back the vines, and shows* **MARY** *the door to the Secret Garden.* **MARY** *wipes her eyes, takes out the key and puts it into the lock, pushes the door open slightly and we have the ...*)

End of Act I

ACT 2

Scene One
Archibald's Dressing Room

(ARCHIE is packing. DR. CRAVEN is pacing. A reader leans against a wall, nearly invisible.)

DR. CRAVEN. What are you doing, Archie?

ARCHIBALD. I'm leaving, Neville. I'm useless here.

DR. CRAVEN. But you must make a decision about Mary. Last night she stole into Colin's room and caused such a disturbance, I had to sedate the boy to get him to sleep. You must send the girl away.

ARCHIBALD. I can't send her away, Neville. She has no one in the world but me.

DR. CRAVEN. Then take her with you.

ARCHIBALD. I can't see her, Neville! When I look at her eyes, it's as if Lily herself were looking back at me.

*(He looks out the window. Or perhaps we see **MARY** on the other side of the stage, looking at the key to the garden.)*

And last night, I dreamed I saw Mary standing right there in Lily's garden. I woke myself up I was so angry. I don't want anyone to go in Lily's garden ever again.

*(**ARCHIBALD** continues packing his bag.)*

DR. CRAVEN.
FROM DEATH SHE CASTS HER SPELL,
ALL NIGHT WE HEAR HER SIGHS,
AND NOW A GIRL HAS COME
WHO HAS HER EYES...

43

DR. CRAVEN. *(cont.)*
> SHE HAS HER EYES.
> THE GIRL HAS LILY'S HAZEL EYES,
> THOSE EYES THAT SAW HIM HAPPY LONG AGO.
> THOSE EYES THAT GAVE HIM LIFE AND HOPE HE'D NEVER
>   KNOWN,
> HOW CAN HE SEE THIS GIRL WHO HAS HER HAZEL EYES.

ARCHIBALD.
> IN LILY'S EYES A CASTLE
> THIS HOUSE SEEMED TO BE.
> AND I HER BRAVEST KNIGHT BECAME,
> MY LADY FAIR WAS SHE.

DR. CRAVEN. *(angry and hurt)*
> SHE HAS HER EYES, SHE HAS
> MY LILY'S HAZEL EYES,
> THOSE EYES THAT LOVED MY BROTHER,
> NEVER ME.
> THOSE EYES THAT NEVER SAW ME,
> NEVER KNEW I LONGED
> TO HOLD HER CLOSE, TO LIVE AT
> LAST IN LILY'S EYES.

ARCHIBALD.
> IMAGINE ME, A LOVER

DR. CRAVEN.
> I LONGED FOR THE DAY
> SHE'D TURN AND SEE ME STANDING THERE

ARCHIBALD AND DR. CRAVEN.
> WOULD GOD HAD LET HER STAY.

DR. CRAVEN	**ARCHIBALD.**
SHE HAS HER EYES,	
	SHE HAS — MY LILY'S HAZEL EYES,
THOSE EYES THAT CLOSED AND LEFT ME	THOSE EYES THAT SAW ME HAPPY LONG AGO.
HOW CAN I NOW FORGET THAT I DARED TO BE	HOW CAN I NOW FORGET THAT ONCE I DARED TO BE

IN LOVE, ALIVE AND WHOLE IN LILY'S EYES, IN LILY'S EYES.	IN LOVE, ALIVE AND WHOLE IN IN LILY'S EYES, IN LILY'S EYES.

(Archibald closes his trunk.)

ARCHIBALD. Now I'll just go see Colin and then...

DR. CRAVEN. No, Archie. You'll wake him.

ARCHIBALD. In ten years have I ever disturbed him?

DR. CRAVEN. I promise you, Archie, as soon as he is well enough, you can talk with him as much as you like. It's just that at the moment...

ARCHIBALD. Then have the carriage brought around. And I'd like a word with Ben, if you can find him.

DR. CRAVEN. And shall I find a school for Mary?

ARCHIBALD. No. I won't send her away.

DR. CRAVEN. *(He tries another approach.)* You wouldn't be sending Mary away, Archie. Only giving her the education she deserves. I feel quite certain that Albert and Rose wouldn't want the girl to grow up just wandering around.

ARCHIBALD. Yes, I see. Well, then...find her a school, Neville. A place where she could learn to dance would be pleasant.

DR. CRAVEN. But when will you be back, Archie?

ARCHIBALD. If it were up to me, I would never see this horrid house again.

*(**ARCHIE** closes his suitcase and heads out the door.)*

Scene Two
In the Gardens

(**MARY** *sits on a stone bench in the gardens. She seems very dejected.* **READERS** *are dejected too.*)

DICKON. Eh up. Hello there, Mary.

MARY. *(clearly unhappy)* Hello there.

DICKON. But why are you in such a bad temper, Mary? Are ye weary of lookin' for a way into that garden?

MARY. No, Dickon. I found the door. And the key. The Robin showed me where it was. But the secret garden is dead.

DICKON. A lot of things what looks dead is just bidin' their time, Mary. Now you tell me exactly what you saw.

MARY. It's cold and gray It's the most forgotten place I've ever seen. With loose grey branches looped all around the trees like ropes or dried up snakes, and dead roots and leaves all tangled up on the ground.

DICKON. But did you have a close look at anything? Did you scrape away a bit of the bark and have a real look at anything?

(She shakes her head.)

Mary. The strongest roses will fair thrive on bein' neglected, if the soil is rich enough. They'll run all wild, and spread and spread 'til they're a wonder.

MARY. *(still very cautious)* You mean it might not all be dead? But how can we tell?

DICKON. Oh, I can tell if a thing is wick or not.

MARY. Wick?

DICKON.
WHEN A THING IS WICK
IT HAS A LIFE ABOUT IT.
MAYBE NOT A LIFE LIKE YOU AND ME.
BUT SOMEWHERE THERE'S A
SINGLE STREAK OF GREEN INSIDE IT.
COME AND LET ME SHOW YOU WHAT I MEAN.

DICKON. *(cont.)*

    WHEN A THING IS WICK
    IT HAS A LIGHT AROUND IT.
    MAYBE NOT A LIGHT THAT YOU CAN SEE .
    BUT HIDING DOWN BELOW
    A SPARK'S ASLEEP INSIDE IT,
    WAITING FOR THE RIGHT TIME TO BE SEEN.

        YOU CLEAR AWAY THE DEAD PARTS
        SO THE TENDER BUDS CAN FORM.
        LOOSEN UP THE EARTH AND
        LET THE ROOTS GET WARM.
        LET THE ROOTS GET WARM.

    WHEN A THING IS WICK
    IT HAS A WAY OF KNOWING,
    WHEN IT'S SAFE TO GROW AGAIN,
    YOU WILL SEE.
    WHEN THERE'S SUN AND WATER
    SWEET ENOUGH TO FEED IT,
    IT WILL CLIMB UP THROUGH THE EARTH
    A PALE, NEW GREEN.

    YOU CLEAR AWAY THE DEAD PARTS
    SO THE TENDER BUDS CAN FORM.
    LOOSEN UP THE EARTH AND
    LET THE ROOTS GET WARM.
    LET THE ROOTS GET WARM
    COME A MILD DAY, COME A WARM RAIN,
    COME A SNOWDROP A COMIN' UP.
    COME A LILY, COME A LILAC,
    COME TO CALL,
    CALLIN' ALL OF US TO COME AND SEE

MARY.

    WHEN A THING IS WICK,
    AND SOMEONE CARES ABOUT IT,
    AND COMES TO WORK EACH DAY,
    LIKE YOU AND ME,

    (spoken)

    Will it grow?

DICKON.

IT WILL.

MARY.

THEN HAVE NO DOUBT ABOUT IT.

WE'LL HAVE THE GRANDEST GARDEN EVER SEEN.

MARY. Oh, Dickon, I want it all to be wick! Would you come and look at it with me?

DICKON. I'll come every day, rain or shine, if you want me to. All that garden needs is for us to come wake it up.

MARY. But Dickon, what if we save the garden and then Uncle Archie takes it back, or Colin wants it.

DICKON. Aye, what a miracle that would be. Gettin' a poor crippled boy out to see his mother's garden.

DICKON AND MARY.

YOU GIVE A LIVING THING,

A LITTLE CHANCE TO GROW.

THAT'S HOW YOU WILL KNOW IF SHE IS

WICK, SHE'LL GROW.

SO GROW TO GREET THE MORNING

FREE FROM GROUND BELOW.

WHEN A THING IS WICK

IT HAS A WILL TO GROW AND GROW.

MARY.

COME A MILD DAY, COME A WARM RAIN

COME A SNOWDROP, A COMIN' UP.

COME A LILY COME A LILAC,

COME TO CALL,

CALLIN' ALL THE REST TO COME

CALLIN' ALL OF US TO COME

CALLIN' ALL THE WORLD TO COME

DICKON.

I PROMISE THERE'S A

SECRET STREAK OF GREEN BELOW

DICKON AND MARY.

AND ALL THROUGH THE DARKEST NIGHTTIME

IT'S WAITING FOR THE RIGHT TIME

WHEN A THING IS WICK, IT WILL GROW.

(**MARY** *takes* **DICKON***'s hand and they walk into the garden.*)

Scene 3
Colin's Room

(COLIN is throwing a tantrum. MARTHA really has her hands full.)

COLIN. Stop looking at me. I hate you! You're horrible and ugly under that haystack you call hair!

MRS. MEDLOCK. *(entering)* Martha! What is going on in here?

(MARY enters.)

MARY. Isn't anybody going to stop that boy screaming?

MEDLOCK. *(seeing MARY)* She is not to go near him, Martha. Those are the Doctor's direct orders.

MARTHA. What can it hurt, Mum? He likes Mary. Let her have a go.

(COLIN throws something at the nurse. She screams.)

COLIN. Get out!

(MARY screams at COLIN. MARTHA, MRS. MEDLOCK and the nurse leave.)

MARY. Colin Craven! You stop that screaming!

COLIN. Get away from me!

MARY. I hate you! Everybody hates you! You will scream yourself to death in a minute and I wish you would!

COLIN. I can't stop! I felt a lump on my back. I'm going to die!

MARY. There is nothing the matter with your horrid back!

COLIN. I'm going to have a lump on my back like my father and die!

MARY. Martha! Come here and show me his back this minute.

MARTHA. I can't, Mary. He won't let me.

COLIN. Show her the lump!

(MARTHA pulls aside COLIN's covers and bedclothes.)

COLIN. Now feel it!

(MARY feels his back.)

COLIN. There!

MARY. No! There's not a single lump there. Except back-bone lumps and they're supposed to be there.

(And now she turns her own back to him.)

See. I have them too.

(MARY grabs his hand and puts it on her back. And then places his hand on his own back for comparison. MARTHA feels her own back and is surprised to find she has lumps too.)

COLIN. *(quietly)* It's not there.

MARY. No, it's not.

(He sits up a little straighter.)

MARY. You were just angry with me for not coming back.

(He doesn't answer.)

Weren't you.

COLIN. Maybe.

MARTHA. I'll leave you two alone, I think.

(MARTHA leaves.)

(MARY turns to some toy or other in his room, determined not to really speak to him until he apologizes.)

MARY. This is nice.

(Finally, COLIN relents.)

COLIN. You're right. I was afraid you weren't coming back.

MARY. I was always coming back, Colin. It just took me longer than I thought because…

COLIN. Because what?

(MARY looks out the window, knowing what it might mean if she tells COLIN about the garden.)

MARY. I found your mother's garden. It's been locked up out there, just like you've been locked up in here, for ten years. Only I found the key. And the other night, I ran out into the storm, and found the door. And now Dickon and I are working on it every day. He says if we clear away all the dead wood, there will be fountains of roses by summer.

COLIN. I didn't know my Mother had a garden.

MARY. You must see it. But Dr. Craven and Mrs. Medlock must never know I've taken you out there, or they will send me away. I'll just go and get your wheelchair and –

COLIN. I can't, Mary. I'll catch a chill if I go. I'll get even worse.

MARY. No you won't. You'll feel so much better. I'll be right back.

COLIN. No, Mary!

(But she is already gone. COLIN *is frightened. He doesn't know what to do or say now.* LILY *appears [or steps out of her portrait] and begins to sing.)*

LILY.

COME TO MY GARDEN,
NESTLED IN THE HILL.
THERE I'LL KEEP YOU
SAFE BESIDE ME.

*(*LILY *comes to the bed, and helps him on with his dressing gown.)*

COME TO MY GARDEN,
REST THERE IN MY ARMS,
THERE I'LL SEE YOU
SAFELY GROWN AND ON YOUR WAY.
STAY THERE IN MY GARDEN,
WHERE LOVES GROW FREE AND WILD
COME TO MY GARDEN,
COME, SWEET CHILD.

*(*MARY *enters with the wheelchair.)*

COLIN. *(sings the counter melody)*
LIFT ME UP, AND LEAD ME TO THE GARDEN,
WHERE LIFE BEGINS ANEW.

*(**LILY** lifts **COLIN** out of the bed and puts him in the wheelchair.)*

COLIN.

WHERE I'LL FIND YOU,

AND I'LL FIND YOU LOVE ME TOO.

*(**LILY** and **COLIN** sing together as **MARY** pushes the wheelchair into the hall, and then into the garden. **READERS** sing with both **LILY** and **COLIN**.)*

COLIN AND READERS.	**LILY AND READERS.**
LIFT ME UP, AND LEAD ME TO THE GARDEN	COME TO MY GARDEN
WHERE LOVE GROWS DEEP AND TRUE,	REST THERE IN MY ARMS
WHERE I'LL TELL YOU,	THERE I'LL............
WHERE I'LL SHOW YOU	SEE YOU SAFELY GROWN
MY NEW LIFE, I WILL LIVE FOR YOU	GROWN AND ON YOUR AND ON YOUR WAY

LILY, COLIN, AND READERS.

I SHALL SEE YOU IN THE GARDEN,

AND SPRING WILL COME AND STAY

TAKE MY HAND AND LEAD ME TO THE GARDEN

COME, SWEET DAY.

(And they enter the garden at last.)

Scene Four
In the Night Garden

(Two other figures appear holding lanterns.)

MARY. Dickon, is that you?

DICKON. Aye, it is, Mary. And Martha, too.

COLIN. Martha, are you surprised to see me outside?

MARTHA. That I am, Master Colin, but just now, you looked so much like your mother, it made my heart jump.

(Now they see the garden.)

COLIN. It's my Mother's garden! It is.

MARY. It's a secret garden. And we're the only ones in the world that want it to be alive.

(They hear a whistle.)

DICKON. Aye, Colin, we'll have you walkin' about and diggin' same as other folk before long.

COLIN. But how can I? My legs are so weak. I'm afraid to –

*(**DICKON** takes over from **MARY** and wheels **COLIN** further into the garden.)*

DICKON. There's a spell in this garden. And the longer you stay in it, the stronger you'll be.

MARY. You must take in long breaths of fresh air. And Dickon has learned some exercises he can teach you.

COLIN. I want to come to this garden every day. I want to live forever and ever!

MARY. You could meet the Robin that showed me this garden. You could help us plant and weed and –

COLIN. Could we, Martha?

MARTHA. Ye could if it were a secret. I could bring ye food out here, if that would help; things me mother makes, oatcakes and ham…But right now we ought to go back inside before they find out you're missing.

(They wheel off the stage in the darkness.)

In the Gardens – On Another Day

(BEN is working in the garden. MRS. MEDLOCK appears.)

BEN. Well upon my word.

MRS. MEDLOCK. Mr. Weatherstaff.

BEN. What do you want? Watch your step there. I'll not have you killin' things willy nilly.

(She steps away.)

Not there. No!

(She steps on something else.)

Stop that. Stand still, woman.

(Finally, she freezes.)

MRS. MEDLOCK. I'm looking for Mary Lennox.

(He doesn't answer.)

I'm sure you've seen her. She's out here all day, I believe.

BEN. What a person believes is no business of mine.

MRS. MEDLOCK. Then have you seen Dickon or Martha?

BEN. Now Dickon I have seen. His mother sent me a poultice for my rheumatics. He's a grand lad, that Dickon. What do you want with him?

MRS. MEDLOCK. That's none of your business, Ben Weatherstaff.

Inside the Secret Garden

(**DICKON, MARTHA, MARY** and **COLIN** are eating a huge picnic. **READERS** are lounging around the garden too.)

COLIN. Oh Martha, can you believe how much I'm eating now. I never liked food before, but when Mary's with me, I do. I've eaten more in this week than in my whole life, I think.

MARY. Dickon. You should've seen the performance Colin gave in the house this morning. Dr. Craven told Colin he was gaining weight and his color was better.

(**COLIN** stops stuffing himself for a moment to laugh, remembering his inspired response.)

COLIN. I told him I felt bloated, and that people who are not going to live often have unnatural appetites.

MARY. But Dr. Craven didn't believe that, of course. He said Colin's father would be very happy to hear of this remarkable improvement.

COLIN. So I flew in a rage. "I won't have my father told!" I said. "It will only disappoint him if I get worse again, and I may get worse this very night. I might have a raging fever. I feel as if I might be beginning to have one right now! You are making me very angry, and you know that is bad for me! I feel hot already!"

MARY. I'm starting to feel rather sorry for Dr. Craven.

COLIN. So am I. He won't get Misselthwaite at all now that I'm not going to die.

MARY. Yes, but it must have been awful to have to be polite for ten years to a boy who was always rude.

COLIN. Am I rude?

MARY. It's always having your own way that has made you rude. But I was that way too, before I began to like people, before I found the garden.

COLIN. What is it about this garden? Is it Magic? Martha, do you believe in magic?

MARTHA. That I do, Colin. And Magic, and charms, and the big good thing by whatever name you call it.

(DICKON *hands him a seedling and a trowel.*)

DICKON. And I believe in these exercises my friend told me about. He said a strong man in a show once showed him how to strengthen his arms and legs and every muscle in his body.

COLIN. Then you must show them to me.

DICKON. But he says tha mun do em gentle at first an' be careful not to tire thyself.

COLIN. I'll be careful, I promise. Dickon, you are the most Magic boy in the world!

DICKON. All right, then. The first thing is this.

(*As* DICKON *begins showing* COLIN *the exercises, the music begins. At first it has a kind of Tai Chi look, using slow movements, as* DICKON *helping* COLIN *begin to move his arms and legs.* MARY *begins to chant.* READERS *begin to learn the exercises too.*)

MARY.

A'O JADU KE MAUSAM
A'O GARMIYO KE DIN
A'O MANTRA TANTRA YANTRA
US KI BIMARI HATA 'O.

(COLIN *can't believe what he's heard.*)

COLIN. Where did you learn that?

MARY. I heard it in India! I'll have to translate, but I know what it means!

(MARY *translates as the underscoring continues. Gradually the music evolves into the main tune, as the action moves into some kind of ritual-like secret charm ceremony. This is really an opportunity for the* READERS *to get involved.*)

MARY. *(cont.)*

> COME SPIRIT, COME CHARM
> COME DAYS THAT ARE WARM
> COME MAGICAL SPELL,
> COME HELP HIM GET WELL.

DICKON.

> COME SPIRIT, COME CHARM,
> COME DAYS THAT ARE WARM.
> COME MAGICAL SPELL
> COME HELP HIM GET WELL

> *(**MARTHA** picks up the Yorkshire version and sings)*

MARTHA.

> COME SPIRIT, COME CHARM,
> COME DAYS THAT ARE WARM.
> COME MAGICAL SPELL
> COME HELP HIM GET WELL.

> *(Now the Spirits and gardeners and **READERS** all sing and begin to dance around them.)*

MARY, MARTHA, AND SOME READERS, (GRP. 1.)	DICKON, ALL OTHERS (GRP. 2.)
A'O	
JADU KE	SPIRITS ALL AROUND
MAUSAM	CHARMS OF EARTH SO NEAR
A'O GARMIYO	
KE DIN	TEND THE SLEEPING BUDS BURIED SAFELY HERE
JADU KE	THAW THE FROZEN GROUND
MAU –	
SAM	LET THE SPRING BREAK THROUGH
A'O	WITH SPIRITS STANDING GUARD
	LIFE WILL COME ANEW

*(**MARY** continues to weave her spell, as all join in singing and dancing around* **COLIN**.*)*

MARY, MARTHA, AND SOME READERS, (GRP. 1.)	DICKON, ALL OTHERS (GRP. 2.)
A'O JADU KE MAUSAM	SPIRITS FAR ABOVE CHARMS ALOFT, ON HIGH
A'O GARMIYO KE DIN MAU - SAM	SWEEP AWAY THE STORMS RUMBLING CROSS THE SKY SPEED THE RISING RUN
KE DIN	MAKE THE BREEZE TO BLOW
A'O	BID THE ROBINS SING BID THE ROSES GROW

*(Now **ALL** sing again, weaving round and around* **COLIN**.*)*

COME SPIRIT, COME CHARM
COME DAYS THAT ARE WARM.
COME MAGICAL SPELL
COME HELP HIM GET WELL.

COME SPIRIT, COME CHARM
COME DAYS THAT ARE WARM.
COME MAGICAL SPELL
COME HELP HIM GET WELL.

COME SPIRIT, COME CHARM
COME DAYS THAT ARE WARM.
COME MAGICAL SPELL
COME HELP HIM GET WELL.

COME SPIRIT, COME CHARM
COME DAYS THAT ARE WARM.
COME MAGICAL SPELL
COME HELP HIM GET WELL.

COLIN. I feel so strong. I feel something new flooding through me, making me so proud, so bold…so tall.

*(**MARY** walks up to him, extends her hand and **COLIN** grasps it. Then with a heroic effort, he tries to stand, but then)*

(He falls. Hard. They rush to him.)

MARTHA. Oh dear lad!

MARY. Colin!

(COLIN looks up from the ground and sees BEN, who has heard their voices entered the Secret Garden.)

COLIN. Who is that man? Go away!

MARY. Colin, it's Ben Weatherstaff, who tends the gardens.

COLIN. Do you know who I am?

BEN. You're young Master Colin, the poor cripple, but Lord knows how you got out here.

COLIN. I am not crippled!

BEN. Then what have you been doing, hidin' out and lettin' folk think you were a cripple. And half-witted!

COLIN. Half-witted!

MARTHA. We'd best be getting in the house. Mrs. Medlock will –

COLIN. Not yet, Martha. I have something to ask Ben. And don't you dare say a word about this.

BEN. I'm your servant, as long as I live, young master.

COLIN. Did you know my mother?

BEN. That I did. I was her right-hand, round the gardens. She said to me once, Ben, if I'm ever ill or if I go away, you must take care of my roses.

(a moment)

When she did go away, the orders was, no one was to come in here. But I come anyway, 'til my back stopped me, about two year ago.

COLIN. I've always been afraid to ask before, but now I want to know how she died.

BEN. *(pointing to the tree)* She was sittin' right there, on that branch. And it broke and she fell and that started her laborin' with you, only the fall had hurt her back. Still, she clung onto life 'til you were born and then she put you in your father's arms and died.

COLIN. So that's why he hates me.

MARY. He doesn't even know you. Wait 'til he finds out you can stand.

COLIN. I don't want him to know anything about this. I don't want anything said to him 'til I can walk. Do you promise? All of you.

(They all join hands and form a circle around him.)

Do you swear by the charm in this garden, that none of you will mention this to my father until I am completely well.

(They all agree, more or less, all at once.)

BEN. That I do.

DICKON. Aye, Colin. Nary a word.

MARY AND MARTHA. I promise.

COLIN. Good then. Take me back to the house, for now.

(piano transition out of scene)

Scene Six

(MARTHA hurries MARY down a hallway.)

MARTHA. Come quickly, Mary. I don't know what they want, but it's Dr. Craven and Mrs. Medlock both, and a mean-looking woman from Scotland.

MARY. That can't be good.

(They open the door to the library, to find DR. CRAVEN taking tea with a severe looking Scottish woman. MRS. MEDLOCK stands to one side.)

DR. CRAVEN. Ah. There's our girl!

(MRS. MEDLOCK and MARTHA withdraw as MARY enters.)

DR. CRAVEN. *(making the intro)* Mary Lennox, this is Mrs. Winthrop, of the Aberdeen School for Girls.

MRS. WINTHROP. Good morning, Mary.

MARY. I don't want to go to a school.

MRS. WINTHROP. Oh, but you do. A useless child never knows her worth, we say.

MARY. My Uncle Archibald said...

DR. CRAVEN. Perhaps if you would tell Mary a little about the school, she'd see she there is no reason to be...

MARY. I won't go. You can't make me.

DR. CRAVEN. Mary Lennox!

MRS. WINTHROP. That's all right, Doctor. This is exactly the type of behavior we are best equipped to handle.

(MARY turns over a table.)

MARY. My Uncle Archibald is the only one who says where I'm going to go and he says I don't have to go to any stupid school!

DR. CRAVEN. She's just frightened, I'm sure.

MRS. WINTHROP. Of course, Doctor. Perhaps she would enjoy seeing some photographs of the girls at their work.

MARY. I hate you! You're a horrible, ugly pig.

DR. CRAVEN. That's quite enough, young lady!

MARY. Your school is a filthy rat hole full of nasty girls and dirty beds. And all anybody really does there is scrub floors!

(She takes a breath.)

I hope you get run over by a train on the way home and your ugly head rolls off in a ditch and gets eaten by maggots!

(another breath)

I hate you! I hate you! I hate you! And if I'm sent off with you, I'm going to bite your arm and you're going to die! Get out of here!

(She throws a chair.)

MARY. Go away! Go away! Go away!

MRS. WINTHROP. Well, we have had one or two cases of this severity.

*(**MARY** stamps on **MRS. WINTHROP**'s foot. Then before **DR. CRAVEN** can stop her, strange Indian music plays, and **MARY** launches into a full blown tantrum, cursing in Hindi, complete with hand signals.)*

MARY.	*(TRANSLATION)*
Mar jaa-o!	*(DIE)*
Baarh me jaa-o	*(GO DROWN IN THE FLOOD)*
Chhoro mujhe!	*(LEAVE ME ALONE)*
Tum barii shaitaan ho!	*(YOU'RE A DEVIL)*

(At the end of the tantrum, she falls on her back, her legs straight in the air, and then her legs fall to the ground with a thump.)

Mar jaa-o!	*(DIE!)*

*(**MRS. WINTHROP** picks up her purse and papers.)*

MRS. WINTHROP. Doctor. What you have here, is a medical problem.

*(**MRS. WINTHROP** exits. **MARY** gets up, feeling quite proud of herself. She turns to **DR. CRAVEN** and curses him.)*

MARY. Chhoro mujhe! I'm going outside.

DR. CRAVEN. *(grabbing her)* You're going wherever I send you, young lady, and right this moment it's into that chair.

MARY. Uncle Archibald said –.

DR. CRAVEN. Oh for God's sake. He doesn't care about you. Why do you think he left without even saying good-bye to you?

MARY. Maybe he was in a hurry.

DR. CRAVEN. You drove him away. You remind him of his wife.

MARY. I look like my Aunt Lily?

DR. CRAVEN. Now it is my task to find you a suitable place to go so that he can return. The other school I have contacted will send no representative. Your bags will be packed and you will leave Saturday week.

MARY. But I can't leave now. Colin needs me.

DR. CRAVEN. The last thing the boy needs is you. Another month of trying to keep up with you and we'll have to put him in hospital, or worse.

MARY. No, you won't. He's much better.

DR. CRAVEN. You have no idea how sick he is. When Colin was born, the midwife didn't expect him to live a week. But I have kept the boy alive for ten years. Only now, thanks to you, he is in grave danger of relapse.

MARY. But you haven't seen how…

DR. CRAVEN. Do you want him in hospital? Do you want him to die?

MARY. To die?

DR. CRAVEN. If Colin is too active at this stage in his recovery, if you push him to take his first step too soon, before his heart is strong enough, he will not survive it. Colin's very life is in your hands.

(She looks away.)

One moment, he could be chatting away, and the next moment, he could clutch at his frail heart and sink to the ground and die.

MARY. And die?

DR. CRAVEN. I will not see the boy in hospital for the rest of his life, or dead before his time. You must go, and go you will. Now that is all I have to say to you.

(**MARY** *cannot answer. But she doesn't leave.*)

DR. CRAVEN. Why are you standing here? Are you quite amused to learn of your power?

MARY. I didn't do anything. You locked him in his room!

DR. CRAVEN. You may go.

MARY. You don't want Colin to get well at all. You want him to die so you can have this house!

(*Suddenly almost out of control,* **DR. CRAVEN** *raises his arm, as though to hit* **MARY**. *Then he stops himself.*)

DR. CRAVEN. *(screaming)* You will leave Saturday week!

(**MARY** *runs from the room.*)

Scene Seven
Mary's Room

MARTHA. Now, in the first place, Mary, you had nothing to do with your Uncle's leaving.

MARY. But…

MARTHA. Your Uncle liked you, I know he did. Didn't he tell you you could have a garden? Didn't he ask you up to his rooms for a chat? Didn't he get you those new clothes and send you books? Well, didn't he?

MARY. But Colin's going to die and it's all my fault.

MARTHA. I think you were just what Colin needed.

MARY. But you're not a doctor, Martha. Will you tell him I didn't mean to hurt him?

MARTHA. You're talkin' like you're already gone, Mary.

MARY. I am gone, Martha. I wish I were a ghost.

MARTHA. No ghost could do what you've done in this house, Mary Lennox.

MARTHA.

WHAT YOU'VE GOT TO DO IS
FINISH WHAT YOU HAVE BEGUN.
I DON'T KNOW JUST HOW, BUT
IT'S NOT OVER 'TIL YOU'VE WON.

WHEN YOU SEE THE STORM IS COMIN'
SEE THE LIGHTNING PART THE SKIES,
IT'S TOO LATE TO RUN, THERE'S
THERE'S TERROR IN YOUR EYES.
WHAT YOU DO THEN IS REMEMBER
THIS OLD THING YOU HEARD ME SAY,
IT'S THIS STORM, NOT YOU,
THAT'S BOUND TO BLOW AWAY.

READERS AND MARTHA.

>HOLD ON,
>HOLD ON TO SOMEONE STANDIN' BY.
>HOLD ON,
>HOLD ON, DON'T EVEN ASK HOW LONG OR WHY.

MARTHA.

>CHILD, HOLD ON
>TO WHAT YOU KNOW IS TRUE.
>HOLD ON 'TIL YOU GET THROUGH.
>CHILD, OH CHILD,

READERS AND MARTHA.

>HOLD ON.

MARTHA.

>WHEN YOU FEEL YOUR HEART IS POUNDIN,'
>FEAR A DEVIL'S AT YOUR DOOR,
>THERE'S NO PLACE TO HIDE,
>YOU'RE FROZEN TO THE FLOOR.
>WHAT YOU DO THEN IS YOU FORCE YOURSELF
>TO WAKE UP AND YOU SAY,
>IT'S THIS DREAM NOT ME
>THAT'S BOUND TO GO AWAY.

READERS AND MARTHA.

>HOLD ON,
>HOLD ON, THE NIGHT WILL SOON BE BY.
>HOLD ON
>HOLD ON, UNTIL THERE'S NOTHING LEFT TO TRY.

MARTHA.

>CHILD, HOLD ON,
>THERE'S ANGELS ON THEIR WAY.
>HOLD ON, AND HEAR THEM SAY,
>CHILD, OH CHILD.......

>AND IT DOESN'T EVEN MATTER IF
>THE DANGER AND THE DOOM
>COME FROM UP ABOVE OR DOWN BELOW,
>OR JUST COME FLYIN' AT YOU
>FROM ACROSS THE ROOM.

MARTHA. *(cont.)*

> WHEN YOU SEE A MAN WHO'S RAGIN'
> AND HE'S JEALOUS AND HE FEARS,
> THAT YOU'VE WALKED THROUGH WALLS
> HE'S HID BEHIND FOR YEARS.
> WHAT YOU DO THEN IS YOU TELL YOURSELF
> YOU KNOW JUST WHAT TO SAY,
> IT'S THIS DAY, NOT ME, THAT'S
> BOUND TO GO AWAY
>
> CHILD, HOLD ON,

READERS AND MARTHA.

> IT'S THIS DAY NOT YOU
> THAT'S BOUND TO GO AWAY.
>
> *(after a moment...)*

MARY. What do you think I should do?

MARTHA. I think you should find a pen and paper and write to your uncle in Paris and tell him to come home. I think you should let Colin's father say whether he likes him standin' or not.

MARY. But why would he listen to me? And what if the letter didn't get to him in time? Dr. Craven said I'm leaving Saturday week.

MARTHA. I'm sure your Uncle will send for you as soon as he sees what you've done for the boy.

> *(getting the paper)*

Now here's some paper, and here's a pen. You do know how to write, I hope. Cause I won't be much help to you in that department.

MARY. A little.

MARTHA. That's all right. You don't have much to say, do you.

> *(**MARY** walks over to the desk and sits down.)*

MARTHA. D-E-A-R.....

MARY.

> ....UNCLE ARCHIE,
> HOW ARE YOU, I AM FINE
> EVERYBODY ELSE IS TOO
> PLEASE COME HOME

> (**ARCHIBALD** *appears, standing on a bridge in Paris.*)

> (*He reads the letter* **MARY** *is writing.*)

ARCHIBALD. Home. I have no home.

MARY.

> MARTHA SAYS YOU'RE IN PARIS.
> IS THAT VERY FAR AWAY?

ARCHIBALD. Not far enough.

MARY.

> DO THEY HAVE NICE GIRLS AND BOYS THERE?
> PLEASE COME HOME.

MARTHA. Now just sign it…

> (*But* **MARY** *turns to* **MARTHA**, *wondering what else she should put in the letter.*)

MARY.

> SHOULD I SAY THAT COLIN'S WELL NOW?

ARCHIBALD.

> – STREETS OF PARIS LIKE A MAZE.

MARY.

> SHOULD I SAY THAT DOCTOR CRAVEN –

ARCHIBALD.

> – SLEEPLESS NIGHTS AND AIMLESS DAYS.

MARTHA.

> I THINK WHAT YOU HAVE IS GOOD.
> LET'S GET IT POSTED, ON ITS WAY.
> HE'LL RUSH HOME, THEN YOU CAN TELL
> HIM ALL THE REST YOU HAVE TO SAY.

MARY.

> OH, KIND SIR, UNCLE ARCHIE,

ARCHIBALD.

> …CAN'T FORGET, CAN'T
> EAT OR SLEEP OR LIVE…

MARY.

WHEN YOU COME INTO THE GARDEN

ARCHIBALD.

CAN'T FORGIVE....

MARY.

PLEASE COME HOME.

YOURS TRULY?

MARTHA.

WELL, MAYBE...

MARY.

SINCERELY?

MARTHA.

WELL, HOW ABOUT...

MARY.

YOUR FRIEND, MARY.

(**MARTHA** *and* **MARY** *exit as we find* **ARCHIE** *standing on a bridge.*)

A Bridge in Paris

(People walk along behind **ARCHIE**. *Finally, a police-man stops. A reader stands on the bridge.)*

OFFICER. Are you all right, Monsieur?

ARCHIBALD. I'm waiting for someone.

OFFICER. Just inquiring if you need some assistance, Monsieur. Something I can do to help you?

(Suddenly, **ARCHIE** *sees* **LILY** *approaching him. She is still dressed as a Spirit, but she seems very real to him, much as she did when they were dancing together. He brightens slightly.)*

ARCHIBALD. No. Thank you. Here she is.

*(***LILY** *comes up to him now.)*

Lily!

(She sings.)

LILY.

HOW COULD I KNOW
I WOULD HAVE TO LEAVE YOU?
HOW COULD I KNOW I WOULD HURT YOU SO?
YOU WERE THE ONE I WAS BORN TO LOVE.
OH, HOW, COULD I EVER KNOW
HOW, COULD I EVER KNOW?

*(***ARCHIE** *takes a big breath and seems to fill himself with her presence.)*

HOW CAN I SAY TO GO ON WITHOUT ME?
HOW WHEN I KNOW YOU STILL NEED ME SO?
HOW CAN I SAY NOT TO DREAM ABOUT ME?
HOW COULD I EVER KNOW,
HOW COULD I EVER KNOW?

ARCHIBALD. With you gone, I don't feel anything, I don't want to feel anything.

LILY.

> FORGIVE ME,
> CAN YOU FORGIVE ME?
> AND HOLD ME IN YOUR HEART.
> AND FIND SOME NEW WAY TO LOVE ME
> NOW THAT WE'RE APART....

ARCHIBALD AND LILY.

> HOW COULD I KNOW I WOULD NEVER HOLD YOU
> NEVER AGAIN IN THIS WORLD, BUT OH
> SURE AS YOU BREATHE,
> I AM THERE INSIDE YOU,
> HOW...COULD I EVER KNOW
> HOW COULD I EVER KNOW.

ARCHIBALD.

> HOW CAN I HOPE TO GO ON WITHOUT YOU?
> HOW CAN I KNOW
> WHERE YOU'D HAVE ME GO?
> HOW CAN I BEAR NOT TO DREAM ABOUT YOU?
> HOW CAN I LET YOU GO?

LILY.

> NOW, YOU MUST LET ME GO.
>
> (**LILY** *takes* **ARCHIE** *by the hand and leads him back to the garden.*)
>
> COME TO MY GARDEN...

Scene Nine
The Garden

(Sparkling spring music begins. It is morning. **MARY** *wheels* **COLIN** *into the garden.* **READERS** *are already there.)*

COLIN. What is it?

*(***DICKON*** *calls to* **MARY***.)*

DICKON. Mary! Come quickly!

COLIN. What is it!

*(***DICKON*** *and* **MARTHA** *enter the garden)*

MARY. It's Spring!

COLIN. But where did it come from?

DICKON. From all our hard work, where do you think?

COLIN. Everything is so…Look at it!

MARY. But where's Ben? He has to see what's happened.

MARTHA. I'll go and fetch him.

*(***MARTHA*** *exits to look for* **BEN***.)*

DICKON. And look at the…

*(***DICKON*** *turns* **COLIN** *round and round in the wheel-chair)*

COME SPIRIT, COME CHARM
COME DAYS THAT ARE WARM
COME GATHER AND SING
AND WELCOME THE SPRING

MARY AND DICKON.

COME, COME
SPIRIT, COME CHARM
COME GATHER AND SING
AND WELCOME THE SPRING

COLIN. Mary! Look at the roses!

MARY. There are fountains of them!

*(***COLIN*** *begins to tease* **MARY***…)*

COLIN. Mistress Mary quite contrary
How does your garden grow…

MARY. I'm not contrary. You take that back.

COLIN. You make me!

(DICKON wheels COLIN behind the hedge, chased by MARY.)

MARY. *(unseen)* I will! I've got you, Colin Craven!

(At just that moment, ARCHIBALD comes into the garden, followed by DR. CRAVEN.)

DR. CRAVEN. Archie. Why didn't you send us a telegram telling us you were coming?

ARCHIBALD. I didn't know, myself, Neville.

(DR. CRAVEN hears the sounds of children shrieking with delight.)

DR. CRAVEN. What on earth is all that…

(COLIN pushes MARY, who is now in the wheelchair, out into the garden with DICKON chasing. MARY squeals with happiness.)

MARY. Colin Craven, not so fast!

DR. CRAVEN. Mary Lennox!

(COLIN stops as he sees his father and DR. CRAVEN.)

COLIN. Father!

(ARCHIE can't believe what he sees.)

ARCHIBALD. Colin?

(COLIN, flush from running and being happy, looks like the healthiest child in the world.)

COLIN. Look at me, Father! I'm well!

(ARCHIE rushes to the boy and clasps him in his arms.)

ARCHIBALD. Oh, Colin, my fine brave boy.

COLIN. It was the garden that did it, Father, and Mary and Dickon, and some kind of…charm that came right out of the ground.

(**ARCHIE** *holds back his tears as he looks at his son.*)

ARCHIBALD. Neville, were you hoping to surprise me with this news?

DR. CRAVEN. Well, of course I knew they were looking better, but I had no idea they were...

COLIN. We didn't want you to know. We were afraid you wouldn't let us come to the garden if you knew.

DR. CRAVEN. But how is it you look so healthy? You haven't touched the food we've sent to your rooms for weeks!

COLIN. Martha brought us food, and we ate in the garden. We ate enough for ten children.

ARCHIBALD. You did, did you.

COLIN. Oatcakes and roasted eggs and fresh milk and...

DR. CRAVEN. It was all terribly confusing. But let me say how happy I am, after all these years, to...

ARCHIBALD. I'm sure it was confusing, Neville. Why don't you take my flat in Paris, and stay as long as you like. And when you return, perhaps you will allow me to help you reestablish your practice, in town if you like, so you can resume your own life, free of the enormous burden you have carried on our behalf.

DR. CRAVEN. Thank you, Archie.

MARY. And you will stay home with us?

(*And* **ARCHIE** *turns to* **COLIN**.)

ARCHIBALD. Colin, Colin. Look at you.

COLIN. It was Ben that kept the garden, alive, Father, until we could get here.

BEN. I knew it was against your orders, sir, but...

COLIN. And it was Dickon who...

ARCHIBALD. Yes, I can imagine. Thank you both. If there is ever anything I can –

(*Then in a sudden moment of quiet,* **MARTHA** *looks down at* **MARY**.)

MARTHA. Sir. What is to become of our Mary?

ARCHIBALD. Why, Mary.

MARY. *(holds out the key)* Here's your key, if you want it back, sir.

ARCHIBALD. I had nearly forgotten you in all this.

MARY. It's hard to remember everybody.

ARCHIBALD. No, it isn't. Three isn't very many people at all. I should be able to remember three people quite easily.

MARY. Would I be one of them?

ARCHIBALD. Mary Lennox, for as long as you will have us, we are yours, Colin and I. And this is your home, and this, my lovely child…

(He opens his arms.)

…is your garden.

*(**MARY** rushes into his embrace and he holds her close as **DICKON** and **MARTHA** clasp hands.)*

*(Then, as **LILY** sings, **MARY**'s parents, approach, saying goodbye to **MARY**, one at a time.)*

ENTIRE COMPANY EXCEPT MARY.

COME TO MY GARDEN,
NESTLED IN THE HILL.
THERE I'LL KEEP YOU SAFE
BESIDE ME…
COME TO MY GARDEN,
REST THERE IN MY ARMS.
THERE I'LL SEE YOU SAFELY GROWN
AND ON YOUR WAY.

LILY AND ALBERT.

STAY THERE IN THE GARDEN,
AS DAYS GROW LONG AND MILD….

*(**ALBERT** exits.)*

*(Then finally, **MARY** and **COLIN** stand with **ARCHIE** kneeling between them as **LILY** sings her goodbye.)*

LILY.

COME TO MY GARDEN.

COME, SWEET CHILD.

(**LILY** *blows them a final kiss. They watch as she goes to her tree and disappears. We hear a single Glissando, hear the chirp of the robin, and see the family embrace in their happiness.*)

The End

OTHER TITLES AVAILABLE FROM SAMUEL FRENCH

GREASE: SCHOOL VERSION

Book, Music and Lyrics by Jim Jacobs and Warren Casey

Musical Comedy / 9m, 9f

Abridged version for school productions

Groups who perform for young audiences or produce musicals with young actors now have an ideal version of *Grease* for their needs. Shorter and more suitable in content for teens and subteens, this abridged version retains the fun-loving spirit and immortal songs that make *Grease* a favorite among rock and roll fans of all ages.

Lightning Source UK Ltd.
Milton Keynes UK
UKOW04f1451240914

239099UK00001B/20/P